Toad makes a road

Russell Punter

Adapted from a story by Phil Roxbee Cox

Illustrated by Stephen Cartwright

Designed by Hope Reynolds
Edited by Jenny Tyler and Lesley Sims
Reading consultants: Alison Kelly and Anne Washtell

There is a little yellow duck to find on every page.

"A new home on a hill!"
croaks Toad with a grin.

She hops to the top.

"I can't wait to move in."

"Penguin's bringing my things.
I hope he comes soon."

Toad hops down the hill.

"There's no road," Penguin moans.
"My old truck will get stuck."

Toad puffs and she pants,
as she pushes her stuff.

"My sore legs," sighs poor Toad.
"Time for bed, that's enough."

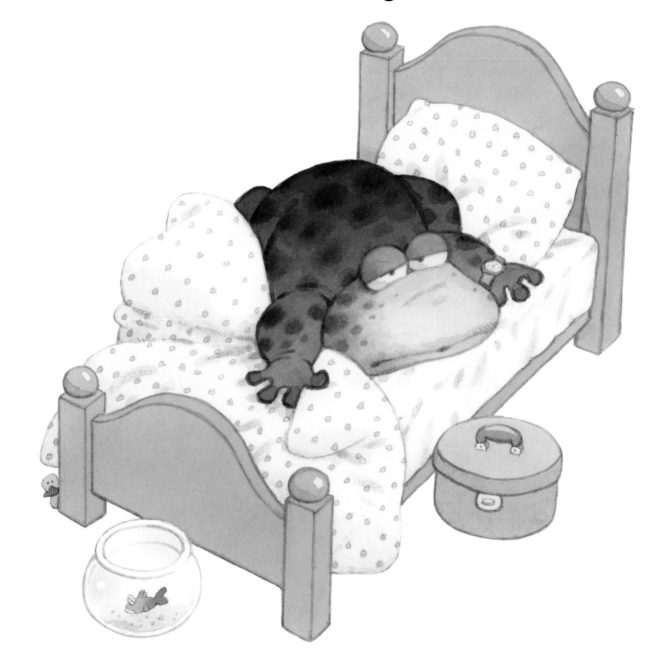

After some rest, Toad is ready for guests.

"My house-warming parties
are always the best!"

But Goat is alone.
"I hope I'm on time?

This hill is so steep
that I had quite a climb."

"I'm sorry," cries Toad.
Then she has an idea...

She finds a big digger,
makes a path for some tar...

then spreads it out smoothly.
Toad smiles. "I'm a star!"

Toad rolls it down firmly.

My road will look fine.

"This is fun," she shouts loudly as she paints a white line.

Soon Toad's road is finished.
She sticks up a sign.

This way to
Toad's place.

Puzzles

Puzzle 1

Can you find the words that rhyme?

Toad	stuck
soon	top
truck	stuff
puff	best
hop	road
rest	noon

Puzzle 2

One word is wrong in this speech bubble. What should it say?

Puzzle 3
Can you find these things in the picture?

Toad   hat

truck   bowl

rug   Penguin

Puzzle 4
Choose the right speech bubble for the picture.

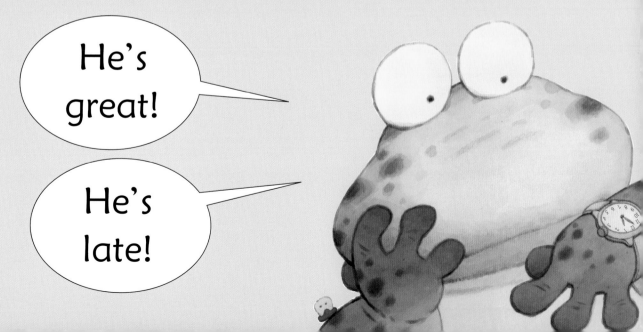

Answers to puzzles

Puzzle 1

Toad ⟶ road

soon ⟶ noon

truck ⟶ stuck

puff ⟶ stuff

hop ⟶ top

rest ⟶ best

Puzzle 2

Puzzle 3

rug

bowl

Toad

hat

Penguin

truck

Puzzle 4

He's late!

About phonics

Phonics is a method of teaching reading used extensively in today's schools. At its heart is an emphasis on identifying the *sounds* of letters, or combinations of letters, that are then put together to make words. These sounds are known as phonemes.

Starting to read

Learning to read is an important milestone for any child. The process can begin well before children start to learn letters and put them together to read words. The sooner children can discover books and enjoy stories and language, the better they will be prepared for reading themselves, first with the help of an adult and then independently.

You can find out more about phonics on the Usborne Very First Reading website, **Usborne.com/veryfirstreading** (US readers go to **www.veryfirstreading.com**). Click on the **Parents** tab at the top of the page, then scroll down and click on **About synthetic phonics**.

Phonemic awareness

An important early stage in pre-reading and early reading is developing phonemic awareness: that is, listening out for the sounds within words. Rhymes, rhyming stories and alliteration are excellent ways of encouraging phonemic awareness.

In this story, your child will soon identify the *oa* sound, as in **toad** and **road**. Look out, too, for rhymes such as **soon** – **noon** and **truck** – **stuck**.

Hearing your child read

If your child is reading a story to you, don't rush to correct mistakes, but be ready to prompt or guide if he or she is struggling. Above all, give plenty of praise and encouragement.